MCR

Trees for the Okapis

by Jorge Aguirre
illustrated by Art Mawhinney

Simon Spotlight/Nickelodeon
New York London Toronto Sydney

Based on the TV series *Go, Diego, Go!*™ as seen on Nick Jr.®

SIMON SPOTLIGHT

An imprint of Simon & Schuster Children's Publishing Division
1230 Avenue of the Americas, New York, New York 10020

Manufactured in the United States of America
0310 LAK
4 6 8 10 9 7 5 3
ISBN 978-1-4169-9090-1

¡*Hola!* I'm Diego. This is my sister Alicia and our friend Baby Jaguar. We're in Africa with some awesome animals . . . the okapis!

Okapis live here in the forest! They can use their long necks and rough purple tongues to pull leaves from tall tree branches, and the stripes on their legs help them to hide! Do you want to play hide-and-seek with the okapis? Great! Come on, *amigos*!

Uh-oh! The okapis can't find anywhere to hide because somebody cut down a lot of trees! Without trees, the okapis won't have enough food to eat and they'll have to find a new home. Will you help the okapis with me? *¡Excelente! ¡Al rescate, amigos!*

We're planting new trees for the okapis' forest. How many trees have we planted so far? Count with me . . . *uno, dos, tres, cuatro, cinco.* Five trees! *¡Cinco árboles!* Come on, let's plant some more!

We have more work to do! Alicia and I are putting up these signs that we made out of old cardboard boxes so that everybody knows that these trees are for the okapis, and that they shouldn't be cut down.

Now Alicia and I are using recycled wood to build a fence around the okapis' home to make it into a nature reserve. The okapis will be safe here. They'll have lots of trees and food to eat inside their reserve.

Look! Now that the okapis are safe in the nature reserve, they want to play their favorite game, hide-and-seek. *¡Vamos, amigos!* Let's play hide-and-seek with the okapis!

All the okapis are hiding behind the trees we planted! I see one okapi eating leaves with her really long tongue! Do you see all five of the okapis?
Great job! You found them!

Yay! We planted trees for the okapis and built a nature reserve where they can live safely. *¡Misión cumplida!* Rescue complete!

Do you want to be an Animal Rescuer, just like me? You can start by visiting a nature reserve or a park near your home to learn all about the animals you see there. The more we know about animals, the more we can do to protect them!

What animals live in this North American nature reserve?

We planted a lot of trees for the okapis, but there are many more animals that need your help—and you don't even have to leave your neighborhood. You can plant flowers and trees to help the animals that live near you!

You can also make signs to protect the animals that live near you, just like we did for the okapis! Make sure to use recycled paper or cardboard. If you see a bird's nest, hang a sign nearby so everyone will know to keep the baby birds safe! Another way to help birds is to hang a bird feeder filled with seeds in your yard or from your back porch. Soon you'll get to watch birds from all over stop by for a snack!

What else can you do to help animals in your neighborhood? Choose one of your ideas and get started today! *¡Al rescate!*